Disclaimer

The following pages contain reinterpretations of myths featuring mythical women from various cultures and traditions. It is important to note that these interpretations are solely the perspective of the author and are intended for creative and speculative purposes only.

The author acknowledges the richness and diversity of mythological narratives across different societies and respects the beliefs and practices associated with them. These reinterpretations do not seek to undermine or discredit any religious, spiritual, or cultural traditions.

Furthermore, it is not the author's intention to cause offense or harm to any individual, group, religion, sect, or community through the exploration and retelling of these stories. Rather, the aim is to offer a fresh perspective and provoke thought and discussion about the roles and representations of mythical women in folklore and mythology.

Readers are encouraged to approach these reinterpretations with an open mind and to engage critically with the material presented. Ultimately, the interpretation of myths is subjective, and differing viewpoints are both valid and welcome.

Thank you for embarking on this journey of exploration and interpretation with an understanding of the author's intentions and a spirit of respect for diverse cultural perspectives.

Acknowledgments

I would like to express my heartfelt gratitude to the following individuals whose love, support, and guidance have enriched my journey in crafting this reinterpretation of mythical women:

To my beloved grandfather (Dada), whose unwavering belief in me gives me wings to fly and pursue all that I desire. Your steadfast support ensures there are no limits to what I can achieve. Your nurturing presence has always been my stronghold, guiding me through every endeavor with love and encouragement.

To my parents, for their unwavering belief in my dreams and their endless encouragement. You have been my pillars of strength, guiding me through life's twists and turns with love and patience. This book is as much yours as it is mine.

To my grandparents (Nana and Nani), whose stories and perspectives have shaped the very fabric of my being. Nani, in particular, I owe a debt of gratitude for opening my eyes to the multifaceted nature of the stories we hold dear. Your insight into the other side of conventional narratives has been instrumental in shaping my understanding of the world. The plethora of stories you shared with me in my childhood has left an indelible mark on my consciousness, fueling my commitment to championing women's voices and empowerment.

To my family, whose collective strength and support have emboldened me to voice my opinions and beliefs in a manner that celebrates the resilience and power of women. Your unwavering belief in me has been the wind beneath my wings.

Thank you, from the depths of my heart, for being my guiding lights on this extraordinary journey.

With love and gratitude,
Aarna

Foreword

Welcome, dear reader, to a journey unlike any other—a journey that traverses the ancient tapestries of myth and legend, infusing them with the vibrant hues of modern interpretation. Within these pages, you will encounter tales of strength, resilience, and transformation, as mythical women from across the ages step forward to claim their voices in a world that has long relegated them to the shadows.

In this extraordinary retelling, the stories of Sita, Athena, Psyche, and Medusa unfold with a modern twist, inviting us to reconsider the narratives that have shaped our collective consciousness for centuries. Guided by the deft hand of our storyteller, we are invited to explore the depths of these timeless myths, unraveling the threads of tradition to reveal new layers of meaning and understanding.

At the heart of these narratives lies a recognition of the enduring power of women—their courage in the face of adversity, their wisdom in times of uncertainty, and their capacity to defy the limitations imposed upon them by society. Through the lens of modernity, we witness the struggles and triumphs of these legendary figures anew, each one speaking to the universal truths that bind us all together.

As we journey through the trials of Sita, the embodiment of virtue and devotion, we are reminded of the complexities of love and sacrifice in a world fraught with injustice and betrayal. Through the eyes of Athena, the goddess of wisdom and warfare, we glimpse the enduring strength of the human spirit in the midst of conflict and chaos. With Psyche, we are drawn into a tale of self-discovery and transformation, where the quest for true love leads to a journey of profound personal growth. And in the haunting visage of Medusa, we confront the dark shadows of fear and prejudice that lurk within us all, challenging us to confront the monsters that dwell within our own hearts.

But this is more than a mere retelling of ancient myths; it is a celebration of the enduring legacy of women throughout history—a testament to their resilience, their tenacity, and their unwavering spirit in the face of adversity. In weaving together the threads of past and present, our storyteller invites us to reimagine the stories that have shaped our world, offering new insights and perspectives that resonate with the challenges of our own time.

As you embark on this odyssey of the imagination, may you be inspired by the courage and wisdom of these mythical women, and may their stories serve as a beacon of hope and empowerment in an ever-changing world. For in the echoes of their voices, we find the strength to rise above adversity, the wisdom to embrace change, and the courage to chart our own course through the vast expanse of human experience.

Story-1
SITA : THE VIRTUE OF ETHICS

In the intricate tapestry of Hindu mythology, the revered figure of Sita, adored by 1.2 billion followers, finds herself ensnared in the intricate threads of paradoxical perceptions. While she stands as a goddess in the pantheon, her character is often cast in the shadows of criticism, particularly by those who champion progressive and feminist ideals. In this cosmic drama, Sita's tale becomes a reflection of the societal struggles embedded in patriarchal traditions. Her purported submissiveness is scrutinized as a consequence of navigating a world where women are confined within the rigid framework of traditional gender roles. Critics argue that her perceived misery is a poignant testament to the erosion of self-identity in the face of oppressive societal norms.

Yet, amidst the echoes of dissent, a chorus of modernist voices emerges within the Hindu community. For them, Sita becomes not merely a victim but a formidable symbol whose influence should be actively challenged. The narrative unfolds as a battleground of ideologies, where tradition clashes with the winds of change, and Sita's character becomes a focal point for reevaluation and transformation. In the contemplative gaze upon Sita, the correlation between femininity and the portrayal of nurturing mother figures comes under scrutiny. Skeptics argue that this association is a subtle manifestation of patriarchal forces seeking to confine women within the restrictive boundaries of societal expectations, denying them the full spectrum of individuality. Thus, in the cosmic dance of mythology, Sita's story emerges as a nuanced exploration of societal dynamics, inviting contemplation and challenging the very foundations upon which her narrative is built. The echoes of her tale reverberate through the ages, prompting introspection on the role of women and the ever-evolving struggle for emancipation within the rich tapestry of Hindu tradition.

The fundamental message of the Ramayana, in both its ancient and contemporary forms, portrays Ram as an ideal king, son, and brother, and even as an ideal spouse until events take a turn for the worst. His selflessness is lauded more and more throughout the epic as it progresses.

Did we forget about the things Sita gave up in her life, even though it is often claimed that "there is a woman behind every successful man"? Is it not reasonable to experience emotions such as sadness and anger in response to sacrifices? Would Ram's life and actions have been so legitimate if Sita hadn't supported him through every stage of his life, every decision he made? Are those the kinds of choices Sita ever wanted to be able to make and put into action? Nobody gives a damn, How could Sita be considered miserable when she was endowed with a prosperous spouse, the throne, and two sons—every available luxury or ambition for a virtuous woman? So here it comes, the story of the goddess. The tale of the deity whose status as a divine is solely due to her sacrifices.

Mithila Naresh-Janak is a king who takes great pleasure in his conquests. Unlike the fruit of previous monarchs, his fruit is the result of his dedication to agriculture. A tall man with a strong build, who likes to cultivate his crops and plow his fields like a regular farmer, even if he is a monarch. His graceful queen Sunanda, wearing a simple silk saree blouse and a veil that billows in the breeze, pats the little jasmine bushes next to it.

Her hair is tied back into a tidy bun as she approaches Janak to examine the freshly tilled field. Her broad, golden-gotta-brimmed tissue ghoonghat shields her lovely, luxuriant skin from the sun. She is a beautiful lady, but her attractiveness goes beyond appearances. She is a dedicated loving wife to her husband and a compassionate queen. She is an expert in the land and everything related to maintaining it. She is knowledgeable about flora and fauna around and appreciative of the offerings of mankind. The couple is known for their kindness and generosity amongst the pupils.

As she walks closer to Janak her veil gets caught between an extended jasmine branch. Tugging and pulling it out she notices that it was caught by a red colour basket floating at the banks of the lazy river. Hesitantly, she approaches the basket and opens the same, by that time the king strode long and is standing next to his wife as she yells in excitement. Her veil becomes entangled in the outstretched branches of a jasmine plant as she draws nearer to Janak. As she pulls and tugs at it, she realizes it is trapped by a red basket floating on the banks of the drifting river. She approaches the basket with some trepidation and opens it up. By this time, the king has made his way over and is standing next to his wife as she shrieks in joy. It had a baby girl in it. They both reared the baby girl inside of it as their own, naming her SITA. They provided her with an inclusive education and showed her a great deal of affection.

As Sita grew older, she transformed into a beautiful and knowledgeable woman. Her eye was drawn to the abundance that the plants provide. She understood which herb or plant would be beneficial to treat a condition and had magical healing abilities. The people of the kingdom highly regarded her because of her healing abilities. Realizing her miraculous abilities, Sunanda raised her spirits and made sure she received pertinent education on the world's floral treasures.

Disregarding the patriarchal societal norms, Janak raised his daughter to be free-spirited. She was boomed when Parshuram presented her with the bow and instructed her to take care of the same. She was the only individual who would be able to move, clean do any chores for the upkeep of the bow. Janak brought up his daughter to be independent by defying patriarchal social conventions.

When Parshuram gave her the bow and told her to take care of the same, she boomed. She was the only one who could keep the bow clean and take care of any maintenance. This reinforced Janak's belief that she was a girl capable of both healing her people and fighting as a warrior for them. He was aware of her unparalleled power compared to all mortals on Earth. He allowed her to pursue her studies and involvement in all royal affairs. Alongside, she was also taught how to become an expert in women's nurturing traits while submitting to the patriarchal system, the happiness of the husband being the virtue of life, maintaining the happiness of the spouse, etc.Sita was raised by two affectionate and empathetic parents. She witnessed at a young age how her parents' affection for one another had enabled them to overcome obstacles and emerge victorious. She had a great deal of faith in humanity, compassion, and generosity. She held the conviction that love and affection were sufficient to surmount any obstacle.

n the hallowed realm of devotion and trials, Sita's unwavering faith encountered its first tempest when Ram, with a brashness that cut through the air like a thunderbolt, shattered Parshuram's bow—a sacred relic to which she had clung with deep reverence since childhood. The bow, a cherished possession, fractured not just in form but in the sanctity it held for her alone. The violation of this cherished symbol, at the very cusp of the swayamvar, kindled a fire of fury within her, burning from head to toe. Yet, in a display of resilience, she masked her ire, refusing to let it consume her. Little did she know, this act marked only the inception of the sacrifices she would make as Ram's devoted wife.

In the early days of their union, she wasn't the queen of Ayodhya, but a maiden enraptured by her chivalrous and divinely perfect husband. Sita willingly bartered her desires, surrendering them to the altar of duty, as she stood steadfastly by Ram's side in his royal obligations.

Forbidden to roam the forest freely, she, the daughter of the woods, found herself confined within the palace walls, with a meager portion of the garden as her sole sanctuary. Her devotion led her to forsake personal aspirations, trading them for the warmth of Ram's adoration. When the call of exile echoed, Sita, driven by an unyielding love, adamantly chose to traverse the arduous path beside her husband. Abandoning regal luxuries, she embraced the challenges of the wilderness, all to preserve the dignity of the man she loved. Yet, the first sting of betrayal pierced her heart when Ram, having rescued her from Ravana's clutches, questioned her purity. The fire of doubt seared her soul as he subjected her to the Agni Pariksha, a trial by fire to validate her innocence.

Having fought wars and conquered realms for her sake, Ram's inexplicable lack of affection cast a shadow over their love. In the wake of his demand for the Agni Pariksha, her love deepened, paradoxically intensified by the astuteness of his request. Sita's tale unfolded as a poignant saga of devotion tested by trials, where each sacrifice etched a chapter in the epic narrative of love, faith, and the profound complexities of the human heart. She couldn't help but wonder what could be pressuring Ram to subject his adored Sita to such atrocities. She was irreparably damaged beyond rescue. Her inner self cried out, "Such atrocity cannot be allowed!"

Throughout the walk to the pyre, she was reminded of how she repelled Ravana at every move he made to protect herself for Rama. In the hopes that this would be the last of his obligations and regulations interfering with their relationship, she underwent the purity test for the sake of his love. It seemed like he valued his responsibilities more than the sacrifices she had made for his affection, and she was reminded of all of them. She understood deep down that he wasn't treating her with dignity, but her love conquered any reservations. Nonetheless, her values battled back, convincing her that going across the raging fire was appropriate. It would enable him to become the virtuous ruler amongst his subjects.

However submissive she may appear walking the pyre was an action that only a strong woman could perform. it wasn't just the duty-bound wife, it was a woman in love. She needed to be exceptionally courageous to go to the fire and then accompany him back to the palace as his wife after he had mistreated her in this way.

Returning home was a difficult time for Sita, a woman whose spouse had required her to undergo a chastity test. She was exposed to rumors and rumors in her vicinity concerning the topic. Attendants and family members would remain mute upon her entrance while constantly chatting about her privately. However, she maintained her conviction in her affection for Ram, being certain that he reciprocated her feelings. She maintained the belief that his love for her exceeded her affection for him and concluded that his being duty-bound was the sole reason he caused her suffering. It was difficult to ignore the above circumstances, but SiyaRam's enchantment at the courthouse each day strengthened her conviction in love and bonded her relationship even further.

Upon Sita's return to her kingdom of Ayodhya, she experienced a notable disparity in the quality of life compared to her time spent in the woods, during which Ram was more consistently there at her side. Soon after having a greater amount of time at her disposal, she came to see the extent to which she had disregarded her aspirations and intellectual pursuits in devotion to the one she saw as her superior. She held him in high regard for his ability to make decisions and manage the almost destroyed realm. Having ample time on her hands, she missed her plants and thought her ability was being squandered. She quickly began providing the staff and maids curative advice, while other people with illnesses came to her for the remedies she could give using herbs and leaves.

She established her garden on the royal grounds and dedicated a great deal of time to tending to the plants and serving those in need. Her contacts with Ram shrunk to their late-night talks during which he filled her up on the day's events, his administration, and the situation in Ayodhya. She believed that her love for him increased over this period as he told her about the choices he made on behalf of his people; he was compassionate and had affection for his pupils. He made just the most responsible and righteous choices for all of them. She was happy for him as he gained popularity as a legitimate monarch, and she felt her love for him increase.

Sita, meanwhile, occupied herself with the day-to-day running of the palace and served as a healer for those in need. Unbeknownst to her, whispers were being shared in her absence, casting doubt on her integrity and chastity. The people of Ayodhya expressed uncertainty regarding her tenure at Ravana's palace, regardless of her pyre walk. Sita was oblivious to the fact that she had become a subject of criticism, seen as an inappropriate role model for a queen. Her acceptance by Ram despite the darkness of her time spent in Lanka in Ravana's palace was viewed as a departure from societal norms, and this led to questioning Ram's leadership as a king. Upon learning about these discussions, Ram secretly instructed his younger brother to escort Sita to the hermitage of Rishi Valmiki and leave her there. Ignorant of the events, Sita regarded the journey as routine, an opportunity to gather medicinal herbs to better serve her people. She packed provisions to last her and Lakshmana for two days, which was typically the duration of such journeys. Sita marveled at the lushness of the jungle, where plants thrived more vibrantly than in her royal garden. She conversed during the trip, while Lakshmana remained serene and unresponsive.

She was happy for him as he gained popularity as a legitimate monarch, and she felt her love for him increase.

Sita, meanwhile, occupied herself with the day-to-day running of the palace and served as a healer for those in need. Unbeknownst to her, whispers were being shared in her absence, casting doubt on her integrity and chastity. The people of Ayodhya expressed uncertainty regarding her tenure at Ravana's palace, regardless of her pyre walk. Sita was oblivious to the fact that she had become a subject of criticism, seen as an inappropriate role model for a queen. Her acceptance by Ram despite the darkness of her time spent in Lanka in Ravana's palace was viewed as a departure from societal norms, and this led to questioning Ram's leadership as a king. Upon learning about these discussions, Ram secretly instructed his younger brother to escort Sita to the hermitage of Rishi Valmiki and leave her there.

Ignorant of the events, Sita regarded the journey as routine, an opportunity to gather medicinal herbs to better serve her people. She packed provisions to last her and Lakshmana for two days, which was typically the duration of such journeys. Sita marveled at the lushness of the jungle, where plants thrived more vibrantly than in her royal garden. She conversed during the trip, while Lakshmana remained serene and unresponsive.

Upon reaching the heart of the jungle, Lakshmana halted the chariot, and Sita couldn't resist inquiring about his calm and serious demeanor throughout the journey. However, Lakshmana remained silent, leaving her puzzled. She asked if his concern was for Urmila, the city of Ayodhya, or the soldiers he was training for the army, but he still did not respond. Eventually, Sita left the chariot to collect medicinal plant seeds she had been eyeing. As she returned, she found their food and provisions spread over a beautiful tapestry and the chariot empty of her belongings.

Confused, she questioned Lakshmana, "Why are we making camp here? My foraging is almost complete, and we can begin our journey back to the city." Finally, Lakshmana broke his silence, informing her that Ram did not want her to return to Ayodhya. She couldn't believe her ears, feeling as if the earth itself had shifted beneath her. Her world seemed to spin. How could Ram, the symbol of love and duty, abandon her without a word or an opportunity for explanation? She tried to convince herself that there must be a valid reason, but her search for one proved futile. She couldn't fathom why he had acted in such a cowardly manner, abandoning his wife without the courage to face her, accusing her of deeds of which she was unaware. It was an injustice beyond belief.

After persistent inquiries, Lakshmana finally revealed the unsettling truths circulating in the city. He explained that the whispers had challenged Ram's duty as a king to maintain Sita as his wife. He said that the rumors had questioned Ram's kingly obligation. Since it was impossible to show she was innocent during her imprisonment in Ravana's palace, Ram felt he had no alternative but to leave her for the sake of justice.

Upon reaching the heart of the jungle, Lakshmana halted the chariot, and Sita couldn't resist inquiring about his calm and serious demeanor throughout the journey. However, Lakshmana remained silent, leaving her puzzled. She asked if his concern was for Urmila, the city of Ayodhya, or the soldiers he was training for the army, but he still did not respond. Eventually, Sita left the chariot to collect medicinal plant seeds she had been eyeing. As she returned, she found their food and provisions spread over a beautiful tapestry and the chariot empty of her belongings.

Confused, she questioned Lakshmana, "Why are we making camp here? My foraging is almost complete, and we can begin our journey back to the city." Finally, Lakshmana broke his silence, informing her that Ram did not want her to return to Ayodhya.

She couldn't believe her ears, feeling as if the earth itself had shifted beneath her. Her world seemed to spin. How could Ram, the symbol of love and duty, abandon her without a word or an opportunity for explanation? She tried to convince herself that there must be a valid reason, but her search for one proved futile. She couldn't fathom why he had acted in such a cowardly manner, abandoning his wife without the courage to face her, accusing her of deeds of which she was unaware. It was an injustice beyond belief.

After persistent inquiries, Lakshmana finally revealed the unsettling truths circulating in the city. He explained that the whispers had challenged Ram's duty as a king to maintain Sita as his wife. He said that the rumors had questioned Ram's kingly obligation. Since it was impossible to show she was innocent during her imprisonment in Ravana's palace, Ram felt he had no alternative but to leave her for the sake of justice. Lakshmana stressed that Ram made an agonizing choice, which is why he found it difficult to talk about with Sita.

However, Sita had already mentally distanced herself from the situation. She was shocked and in utter disbelief. She couldn't fathom that she had relinquished everything and loved a man for whom she held no significance compared to his duties as a ruler. She had been a silent, devoted, yes-man partner to Ram even in the most difficult situations in life. Her love was her commitment to Ram irrespective of the situation.

In her thoughts, she pondered how the Raja Ram had conquered her husband Ram, but she had never married the ruler. Ram was her husband, and she couldn't comprehend why his duties as a husband had been forsaken. Lost in her turmoil, she continued to walk, deaf to Lakshmana's calls and the world around her. She could not get off the chaotic carousel that was her thoughts, and she continued to walk until she was out of sight. Devoted to serving his king, Lakshmana left in despair. She struggled to believe that she had given her everything to love him, given up all she wanted, and given up her hopes and desires to win his love.

He, the epitome of justice, had removed all marital responsibilities and duty towards her, while she had considered him and her duties towards him to be the most important purpose of her existence. She was overcome with self- loathing for bearing suffering for Ram. She swore solemnly to never love him again, not realizing that to not love him would be to erase her existence since her love for Ram was unconditional and pure, the essence of who she was. Nonetheless, she yearned to overcome her emotions and banish any thoughts of Ram.

Time lost meaning, and day and night merged into a sense of hope-lessness. She forsook food and water, moving in aimless circles, until her strength waned, and she collapsed onto a bed of Senna leaves. That was the day when Sita left the thought of being beside Ram, and very rougefully the world never speaks of any of this part in Ramaya-na. The later half "Uttar- Ramayana" also speaks of the bravery and intellect of her sons- Luv & Kush. but nothing is spoken of the most virtuous pious Hindu goddess, who blatantly followed her husband through thick and thin to be abandoned in the end. Once full of love her heart by the end was a stone figure.

That was the day Sita gave up on the idea of being at Ram's side, and ironically, no one ever discusses this portion of the Ramayana in the world. The courage and intelligence of her sons, Luv and Kush, are also mentioned in the latter part of "Uttar-Ramayana." However, little is spoken about the most honorable and devout Hindu goddess, who openly supported her husband through good times and bad until being abandoned in the end. Her heart was a stone figure in the end, once full of love.

Story-2

PSYCHE : TO LOVE & TO TRUST

Psyche stood there alone, begging him to come back but his cold stares haunted her and his voice echoed in her mind – 'to love is to trust, I wanted you to love me & not my beauty or wealth, for I am Eros the son of Aphrodite". Alas! Why was destiny so cruel, why did she not trust her own judgment? She cursed herself, wept her heart out, and wandered around in her lonely palaces. The beautiful jewel-studded ivory bed or the grand gardens looked sullen and grey. She kept running, sprinting away from herself, across the mountains and amidst the clouds. She could smell him in the air, but he will never come back.

In the hallowed annals of Greek mythology, the profound narrative of Eros and Psyche stands as a testament to the enduring hope that love can conquer the darkest of evils. Eros, the son of the enchanting Aphrodite, embodied not just love but the very essence of desire. His divine duty was to unleash arrows upon unsuspecting hearts, igniting the flames of love within. In the mortal realm, Psyche, a captivating young woman, became the embodiment of the human spirit, radiating a beauty that transcended time.

Psyche's allure, however, became a double-edged sword. The world, enraptured by her beauty, turned against her, prompting a relentless pursuit of true love that extended beyond superficial attraction. She felt herself to be the fairest among three sisters, pride and charm woven into her appearance. Yet, she came to recognize that her undeniable beauty was both a blessing and a vulnerability. Men admired her from a distance, respecting and looking up to her, but the prospect of forging a romantic connection with the captivating Psyche remained elusive.

As Psyche navigated the complexities of love, her father, burdened by concern, sought guidance from the Oracle of Delphi. The prophecy unveiled a destiny adorned in shadows – a hill veiled in black would be the stage for her union with a spouse, described as the "evilest of the evil" and a "monstrous serpent."

Dread clutched Psyche's heart as she awaited her mysterious suitor in the shrouded silence of a dark night.

Abruptly, the wind spirited her away to a magnificent mansion, enveloped in happiness but obscured by the impenetrable darkness. Fearful of the doom that love might bring, Psyche refrained from laying eyes on her elusive spouse, a figure who vanished into the woods before dawn and returned late at night. His face remained veiled in mystery, yet she yearned desperately for his affection.

In the cocoon of bliss before her sisters' arrival, Psyche's life unfolded in idyllic splendor, unaware of the impending challenges that would unfold in her journey of love.

Her sisters, who were envious of her lavish lifestyle and abundant affection, ruined her happiness by revealing the second part of the prediction. She was determined to see his face tonight. They were successful in their efforts to plant doubt in her mind. The light cast by the candle showed her husband to be the exact opposite of a monstrous creature: a handsome adult male. That lighted candle brought darkness back to her existence as Eros abandoned her owing to suspicion. The paths and roads of trust that love takes are indescribable. Since he couldn't trust her, eros had to leave his mind before any atonement could be accomplished. Not knowing what to do, she has been frantically crossing land and water to find her husband and apologize for her foolish decision to mistrust him.

She stopped in her stride as the most exquisite temple appeared before her. She stepped into the temple, and there, standing before her, was a divine lady, her hair tousled up over her shoulders and as white as froth. Her husband's mother, Aphrodite, was honored in the temple. She felt a little wave of relief wash over her for the first time. She sobbed, "Mother, I am your son's adored, but alas, he has left me owing to my folly. Please forgive me, Mother, and welcome me back into the family after I listened to my sisters and questioned our love.

Your son left without a word, leaving me in misery. When Aphrodite saw her, she lifted her up and scrutinized her.

And it came roaring back with a vengeance. The goddess of love and beauty, Aphrodite, had her attention diverted by the beautiful Psyche, sister of Aglaura and Cidippe. She was the girl who had made the goddess of love and beauty exhibit envy & jealousy when she directed her son Eros to make her fall in love with him and change her into a love-struck creature for the worse. Since the birth of the psyche, Aprodite's renown and popularity among people of all ages had declined, and she wished to see her destroyed. The stories of her beauty were all true and her foolish son, instead of killing her, had fallen in love with her. She was full of anger and jealousy. With one look at her, Aphrodite knew she was Venus' love child with the God of humanity. The dishonesty of her son shocked Aphrodite beyond belief. Her son had married the kind of woman that she abhorred. But a chilling joy at her abandonment crept over her demeanor. But a chilling joy at her abandonment crept over her demeanor. She finally got what she'd been wanting for a long time. She realized that Psyche could simply be destroyed by her own hands. While Psyche pleaded with Aphrodite to convince her son to accept her again, Aphrodite, obsessed with envy considered the most challenging challenges she could offer her to show that she was appropriate for her son. Aphrodite was determined to punish this soulful girl, like others, she was intimidated by her beauty. Psyche must die. She thought, "My son is only mine, he will not be able to stay away from her for so long."

"AH! My Sweet Girl" She looked down while staring at Psyche. Psyche began to cry. She finally found some peace in sobbing in front of her husband's mother; she felt like family. She had no idea that Aphrodite had devised a devious strategy to hasten her demise by playing a game of wits with her.

Using her most soothing expressions, Aphrodite spoke, "Shush, shush," but who am I to welcome you in our home? You married my son and lived with him for so many days on your own, and now you come to me?" She inhaled deeply before spewing her venom: "You chose to invite your jealous sisters to the splendid home built by my son for you & not me?" The question then becomes, "But why should I help you?" She made fun of Psyche.

Psyche's feelings of remorse and despair prevented her from seeing any malice in the questions. She knelt down on the floor, broken by her sins and regret, and cried out to her mother, "But you are my mother now, and I know I have been a bad daughter, but I am ready to repent and do your bidding, pls accept me and ask your son to have mercy on me.?"

Aphrodite sighed, "Well, well, such a pity; Now that you talk about the virtues of motherhood, let me indeed be a mother to you and train you to be a good worthy daughter and wife." Aphrodite's efforts are being put into motion; she is certain this time that she will emerge triumphant.

She followed Aphrodite up a hill covered with fields of various crops, including wheat, poppies, millets, sesame, and many more. Knowing that no human soul could complete and that it would exhaust her to the point where she would forget about ever seeing Eros, Aphrodite deliberately set out to do the job. To further ensure there was no chance of success, she proposed a strict time limit. I want you to sort these seeds into good and bad by this afternoon, as befits a decent daughter and mother. Aphrodite said, "If you don't, I'll never let you see Eros again."

Psyche's eyes widened in despair; she had no idea how to sort through so many small seeds. She knew that if she took on this challenging work, she would never see her partner again.

She lay on the ground, feeling numb and ready to die as she recalled her first and final glimpses of Eros. Opening her eyes, she saw she was above a colony of ants. Feeling awful for crushing a colony of ants with her weight, she remembered her nanny's advice to treat even the smallest animals with kindness and feed them some grains and water. The ants were relieved and happy with her, so she told them her tale when they inquired what was wrong. How she was born gorgeous, but nobody ever liked her because they were afraid she would steal the spotlight from them. She told the ants how her husband loved her so much that he never let her see his face, but instead wanted her only to feel his love and trust her intuition until the moment was perfect, at which point he would unveil himself. She berated herself for believing her sisters, betraying her husband's word, and mistaking her spouse for a monster who didn't want to show himself. How horrible that she had considered murdering her spouse. And now, since he had abandoned her, her mother-in-law had assigned her to sort the grains on the hill. The realization that she could never complete this work and, hence, never see her spouse again left her feeling helpless and demotivated to continue living. She felt terrible about what she'd done, therefore, the ants were sympathetic and offered to assist. who recognized the movement of grains better than ants? Pleased by her compassion for them, they resolved to aid her. They banded together and got to work, eventually splitting off from the mother dune to generate numerous smaller dunes, each with a unique seed.

When Aphrodite saw the separated heaps, her fury had no boundaries, and she became enraged. She had a hard time believing that Psyche was capable of doing this. Her rage swelled to epic proportions. Now she had to devise a challenge that Psyche could not only not do but also would put her life in danger if she tried. She had no desire to look at her in the face ever again. She called upon Psyche, and Psyche led her to the mountain's summit from where River vestige came. The sound of the river was resonant, much like the sound of machinery and business.

The water came crashing down from an enormous height with incredible force and power. She gave Psyche the order to descend to the waterfall's base, and she asked her, "Psyche, do you see those dark waters of the river Estige?" Fill this bottle with its water; a married lady should understand the significance of carefully regulating the flow of the tide at all times".

After reaching the waterfall, Psyche saw that the rocks in the area were dangerous since they were steep and covered with ice spikes that resembled blades. In the middle of the turbulent river that was pouring over inaccessible towering cliffs that could only be navigated by winged beings, the gods nervously watched Psyche's precarious position. They were aware of the possibly deadly nature of the responsibilities that Aphrodite had placed upon her, and therefore they were concerned for her safety. Even though they were concerned for the beautiful soul that was being subjected to severe consequences, their ability to intervene was restricted since Aphrodite was so set on bringing about Psyche's death. When confronting the dangerous gorges at the waterfall, where surges of spiky water threatened to wipe out her, Psyche, who was propelled by her love for Eros, found strength in her unwavering resolve, and her determination made the danger seem trivial. Amid the stinging winds, she wished for the ability to fly, and this realization prompted her faithful eagle to answer her call with a sharp whistle. The gods let out a collective sigh of relief when the eagle, in a surprising demonstration of comprehension, flew to the dangerous water, filled Psyche's bottle with it, and brought it back to her.

The gods saw some hope when the eagle brought the water, but Aphrodite, the goddess of beauty, was so furious with Psyche's unlikely achievements that she went beyond all limits.

She informed her that other creatures were assisting her in doing her chores and that in her son Eros's eyes, that was not creditable. Never trusting Psyche to overcome obstacles she thought too great, she gave up all kindness and gave Psyche a box to go to the Underworld. Assigned the duty of capturing a sliver of Persephone's beauty, Aphrodite saw this as Psyche's last demise, undervaluing her innocence. Aphrodite foresaw Psyche's demise as her loveliness drained away in the box.

Nevertheless, Psyche followed the road to Hades while thinking back on Eros and their special times together. Knowing that the road she was on would not be reversed, love drove her on as she made her way towards the gates of death. Entering the gates and crossing the river to the afterlife, she paid Charon with all she had to go to Persephone's gloomy castle. Psyche set out into the dark valley, lit only by a weak candle, determined to face the trials that awaited her in the land of the dead.

Seeking Persephone in the shadowy palace, Psyche drew back from mirrors and wall murals depicting an eerie tale of death. She turned to face Persephone and told her that Aphrodite had requested that she empty the casket of her beauty into the box. Persephone was equally astounded by this human's perseverance in pursuing her desire for Eros, given that she had entered the realm of the dead and begged the Queen of Dead to strip away her beauty so it could be presented to her mother-in-law, who was clearly indifferent to her daughter-in-law. Persephone complied with Aphrodite's demand. Psyche paled and her bones began to show through her gorgeous face as she allowed her to drain all of her splendor until she could no longer bear the agony. Her cries echoed across the sky, punishing the gods for their incapacity to intervene and save a pure spirit. After this event, Persephone knew she be ugly and damaged for all of eternity. Persephone gave the box back to Psyche when she recovered consciousness, and she saw that the poor girl was still grinning at herself for doing the job and for perhaps winning her partner back.

Hermes took quick measures to guarantee that Eros was present in his mother's garden, which was the location where his mother was publicly shaming and berating Psyche. After leaving his room, he saw Psyche lying weary in the yard of his mother's house. When he saw her in that pitiful position in his mother's garden, he was unable to prevent the love he felt for her from motivating him to take action. He no longer had feelings of betrayal because he was, and this allowed the wound caused by betrayal to heal. Eros was moved and comprehended the love Psyche had for him at that moment. He made the decision to give her another shot at finding love.

As Eros and Psyche reunited, the flames of their love intensified, forging an unbreakable bond. In a tender moment, Psyche implored Eros to extend forgiveness to his mother for the transgressions she had committed. The tale of Cupid, the embodiment of desire, and Psyche, the soul entwined in love, unfolds before us, revealing the resilience of a man captivated by desire and a woman overcoming adversity to discover love and happiness. This narrative of enduring devotion emerges as an immortal saga destined to be recounted for generations to come.

Yet, amidst the celestial romance, a shadow lingers—an ancient myth echoing the haunting notion that a woman's suffering carries the spectral weight of another. This profound thought, deeply etched in collective awareness, adds a nuanced layer to the tale of Eros and Psyche, reminding us that within the realms of love, echoes of sacrifice and endurance resonate across time.

Story-3
KAIKEYI : LAST OF HER NAME

As my grandmother led me through the latest retelling of the Ramayana, I found myself contemplating the timeless nature of its characters. Remarkably, despite the countless reinterpretations, Ram remains the embodiment of righteousness and courage, Laxman unwaveringly faithful, and Sita eternally upholding her piety and dignity. Yet, in the midst of these revered figures, one character often overshadowed by a singular mistake emerges as an intriguing and relatable figure: Kaikeyi.

Our society tends to brand individuals as irredeemable based on a single misstep, a harsh reality that Kaikeyi too faced. Her one mistake cast an unwarranted shadow over her entire life, reducing her to the malevolent queen. Unfortunately, her numerous virtues and talents went unnoticed amidst the portrayal of her as the quintessential antagonist.

Kaikeyi was far from perfect, but her brilliance was exceptional. In a time when women were predominantly valued for their beauty, serenity, and obedience, she stood out as a unique blend of beauty and intelligence. From a young age, Kaikeyi immersed herself in manuscripts and weaponry, mastering skills that surpassed the understanding of many of her contemporaries. The only daughter of Ashvapati, she was raised to be strong, independent, and unapologetically bold. Her proficiency in archery rivaled that of seasoned warriors, and her knowledge spanned diverse subjects. Kaikeyi was not just beautiful; she possessed a rare intellect that set her apart. Her milky white skin, radiant like gold, only complemented her extraordinary talents. In essence, she was a woman ahead of her time, a combination of beauty and intelligence rarely found in the world.

The roots of Kaikeyi's unconventional character traced back to her upbringing. Her father, Ashwapati, possessed the unique ability to comprehend bird language, a gift with a perilous condition: revealing his knowledge would cost him his life.

A chance encounter with two conversing swans led to a revelation that prompted the queen's insistence on knowing the details, even at the risk of the king's life. This perceived indifference led to her exile from the kingdom, leaving Kaikeyi without a maternal presence during her formative years.

Raised amidst seven brothers, Kaikeyi's feminine influence came from her caretaker, Manthra, a woman more cunning than nurturing. While Manthra imparted survival skills, she failed to instill the value of self-sacrifice for victory, encouraging Kaikeyi to fervently pursue what she believed to be just and fair.

In reconsidering Kaikeyi's narrative, it becomes clear that beyond her portrayed flaws, she was a woman of remarkable depth and substance, challenging societal norms and expectations with her intellect, talents, and unwavering determination.

Ashvapati, Kaikeyi's father, had nurtured her in the wilderness, where she honed her exceptional hunting skills and navigated the jungle with ease. During a routine hunting expedition, she stumbled upon a prince ensnared by a formidable beast, his life hanging in the balance. With precision and skill, she felled the beast, rescuing none other than King Dasharatha himself.

Amidst the adrenaline of the rescue, Kaikeyi couldn't help but be struck by the king's regal presence and undeniable allure.

Impressed by Kaikeyi's bravery and archery prowess, Dasharatha sincerely proposed marriage. Ashwapati, her father, welcomed the proposal but believed in offering Kaikeyi a unique young adulthood. The decision rested in Kaikeyi's capable hands. After a night of contemplation, she, like a wise woman, graciously accepted Dasharatha's proposal, expressing not just a desire for marital union but also a commitment to nurturing and enhancing her extraordinary gifts.

Kaikeyi, far from being a passive queen, emphasized her wish to delve deeper into politics and combat. Dasharatha, respecting her ambitions, promised discreetly continued studies post- marriage and welcomed her caretaker, Manthra, to Ayodhya. This arrangement cemented their relationship on a foundation of mutual respect.

Their marriage was characterized by partnership rather than submission. Kaikeyi's identity remained intact, and she proved to be a woman of integrity, true to her word. Her quiet training sessions and contributions to Dasharatha's decision-making process showcased the strength of their bond.

Despite Dasharatha's subsequent marriages, Kaikeyi retained her favored status, acknowledging and supporting his regal decisions. As the queens bore sons, Kaikeyi's love for Ram surpassed even her affection for her own children, a testament to her exceptional stepmotherly devotion.

Kaikeyi's prowess extended beyond the court. In a losing battle, she skillfully aided Dasharatha's escape, earning her two boons that would later shape the course of the Ramayana. Her active involvement in governance and court processes, concealed from plain view, contributed to Ayodhya's prosperity and Dasharatha's admiration for her.

As the boys grew, Kaikeyi continued to play a vital role, keenly observing Ram's exceptional qualities. While recognizing his potential for greatness, she also foresaw potential challenges in his leadership style. Her unique insight into Bharat's administrative skills led her to plan a strategy favoring him as the true king.

Kaikeyi, driven by concern for Ayodhya's well-being, envisioned a realm led by Bharat's administrative prowess, with Ram and Lakshmana as unparalleled warriors. Despite the difficulties she anticipated, she remained optimistic that Dasharatha would eventually understand and support her cause.

Her deep involvement in Ayodhya's governance, dedication to her sons' growth, and awareness of Ram's destiny in the cosmos portrayed Kaikeyi as a woman of foresight. Her anticipation of Ram's exile, coupled with her unwavering love and support for him, reflected a mother's sacrifice for a greater purpose.

However, as the impending coronation of Ram approached, Kaikeyi's actions took an unexpected turn. Influenced by Manthra's counsel on the necessity of Ram's exile for the greater good, Kaikeyi abandoned her earlier support for the coronation. The consequences of her decisions, including Dasharatha's unintentional demise and Bharat's resentment, weighed heavily on her.

Choosing mourning attire over regal robes, Kaikeyi entered the kop bhavan, concealing her despair. In this secluded chamber, she requested the boons granted by Dasharatha, unaware that this request would set off a tragic chain of events. Her sorrow had deeper roots than apparent, stemming from the pain of sacrificing her son's potential happiness and the looming judgment of future generations. In a moment of heart-wrenching vulnerability, Kaikeyi's actions, driven by love and a sense of duty, sealed her fate. As Ram embarked on his exile, Kaikeyi remained secluded, weeping for the sacrifices made, the unspoken truth of her motives, and the irreversible consequences that unfolded.

Kaikeyi found herself grappling with the weight of her choices as Ram, Sita, and Lakshman sought her blessing in the kop bhavan before embarking on their journey into the jungle. Seeing Sita, now a newly-wed, clad in plain cotton instead of the royal splendor she deserved, pierced Kaikeyi's heart. Yet, amidst the pain, Ram's continued politeness as he sought her blessings revealed his ability to see beyond her perceived villainy, offering a glimmer of solace.

Nevertheless, the rest of the world had branded her the archvillain.

The departure of Ram threw Ayodhya into disarray, exacerbated by Bharat's refusal to assume the throne. Dasharatha, overwhelmed by the pain of separation, succumbed to sorrow, plunging the nation into an abyss of despair from which it could not emerge. The aftermath of Kaikeyi's decisions cast a profound impact on her life.

In the wake of Ram and Dasharatha's deaths, the people of Ayodhya directed their grief and anger toward Kaikeyi. Shunned from the palace, she endured a solitary existence, isolated from the kingdom she once called home. Despite Ram's instructions to Bharat to treat her with respect, Kaikeyi grappled with loneliness and the weight of public disdain.

Kaikeyi, however, refused to let her past dictate her future. Determined to seek forgiveness, she approached Ram, finding understanding in his gaze. Her efforts to win over Bharat, unfortunately, proved futile, leaving her wrestling with feelings of inadequacy as a mother. Despite witnessing Ram's triumph over Ravana, forgiveness eluded her, a deep disappointment she carried with her.

One decision had overshadowed Kaikeyi's entire life, casting her as the perpetual antagonist in the Hindu narrative—the stepmother whose actions led to the great ruler's exile from Ayodhya for 14 years. The world failed to see her genuine remorse, attempts at redemption, and her success in gaining Sita's forgiveness. The mystery persisted as to why the world insisted on perpetually vilifying her.

Yet, amidst the darkness, there were unintended benefits to her actions. The exile of Ram set in motion a series of positive outcomes—Ahilya's liberation, Shabri's happiness, the end of Ravana's tyranny in Lanka, and peace between Bali and Sugriva. Despite these unintended benefits, Kaikeyi remained forever cast as the arch-nemesis in the tapestry of Hindu epics.

Story-4

MEDUSA : POISON IVY

Standing at the propylon, My eyes lock hers as I cry,
Oh yeh, I see some sympathy,
Before misogyny piles on.
Oh yes, I was the virgin, how could she not have seen, Spare the male
and curse me, for the deeds were only me!

In the sacred courtyard of Athena's temple, Medusa stood, her eyes
reflecting a turbulent river in full spate. The divine encounter with
Poseidon within the temple's hallowed halls had left her convinced
that Athena, the goddess of beauty, bore witness to the unholy liaison
through a nearby window. As she collapsed under the weight of pain
and humiliation, she clung to the hope that Athena would intervene
and rescue her. However, her pleas echoed in vain, and she found
herself abandoned in her desperate wait.

Once a figure of allure with hair like threads of gold, Medusa now
stood barefoot on icy rocks, her once-lush locks ravaged. The aftermath had drained her coping mechanisms, leaving her weakened
and despondent. Athena's gaze, rather than offering solace, deepened her sense of despair. As she observed Athena approaching, any
flicker of hope within Medusa's heart was extinguished.

Athena stormed out of the temple just as Poseidon made his exit, fury
emanating from her eyes. Accusing Medusa of sacrilege, Athena
berated her for violating the vows of chastity she had taken as a
priestess. Athena's anger echoed through the sacred space, oblivious
to Medusa's suffering and the turmoil that had unfolded. The wrathful
goddess, consumed by the fear of setting a bad example, failed to
recognize the agony etched on Medusa's face.

Bewildered by Athena's rage, Medusa longed for empathy rather than
anger. However, Athena's focus was solely on blaming Medusa, oblivious to the broader context. The thunderous storm

outside mirrored the tempest within the temple, drowning out Medusa's confusion. Athena, driven by societal norms and the fear of divine retribution, placed the blame squarely on Medusa's shoulders. Athena's selective condemnation stemmed from a combination of fear and adherence to patriarchal standards. The male deity, Poseidon, went unquestioned in his transgressions, while Medusa bore the weight of blame. The societal tendency to blame women for their own victimization perpetuated the injustice further. Athena, caught in a moment of rage, cursed Medusa with a fate so severe that it sent shivers through the atmosphere.

As Athena spoke the curse, the elements seemed to align with the impending doom. The atmosphere turned ominous, and the very air whispered of impending catastrophe. Medusa, still oblivious, could only watch as the curse unfolded. Athena's curse, turning Medusa's once-golden hair into venomous serpents, left her in a state of shock. The transformation was accompanied by a cacophony of hissing snakes, a terrifying symphony of retribution.

Medusa, now bearing the curse of turning any who gazed upon her into stone, felt the weight of her transformation. Her once-beautiful appearance was replaced by a terrifying countenance. Yet, as she grappled with her altered self, a newfound strength emerged. Her serpentine hair, an extension of her newfound power, responded to her thoughts. Medusa, now a symbol of vengeance, turned away from Athena, leaving the temple with an air of sinister determination.

Unbeknownst to Medusa, the gods observed her transformation with trepidation. Athena, cursed to avoid direct eye contact with Medusa, pondered the consequences of her actions. Medusa, now an embodiment of evil, ventured into the world, leaving behind a trail of fear and devastation. The gods, recognizing the danger she posed, sought to quell the threat by sending armies to subdue her.

Despite their efforts, Medusa proved to be an unstoppable force. Her ability to turn living beings to stone thwarted every attempt to bring her down. The gods, fearing the havoc she could wreak upon the world, turned to Perseus, a demigod with divine assistance, to put an end to Medusa's reign of terror.

Perseus, armed with gifts from various gods, embarked on a mission to slay Medusa. With Athena's mirror shield, Zeus's sword, and Hades' invisible helmet, Perseus faced the Gorgon. The gods, driven by the need to contain the menace they had unleashed, watched as Perseus succeeded in severing Medusa's head.

Athena, recognizing the gravity of her actions, underwent a transformation of her own. Medusa's severed head became a symbol of bravery on Zeus's shield, depicting the goddess facing the horrors she herself had unleashed. Medusa's curse turned her into a cautionary tale, a reminder of the consequences of unchecked rage and the need for empathy.

As time passed, Medusa's story evolved into a narrative used by mothers to teach their children about the battle between good and evil. Yet, the underlying trauma and hardship Medusa endured before her transformation often went unnoticed. The cultural norm of pitting women against each other, prevalent even in this mythical tale, reflected the sexism ingrained in society.

Medusa's story, from a victim of divine misconduct to a symbol of vengeance, serves as a reflection of the complexities within narratives of power, justice, and victimhood. Her journey, fraught with pain and transformation, invites contemplation on the consequences of unchecked anger and the importance of empathy in the face of suffering.

Story-5
ATHENA -I (AI) : GREY IN COLOUR

AI is designed to process vast amounts of data, learn from patterns, and generate insights, often contributing to informed decision-making, which all seems inspired by the Greek goddess Athena, renowned for her wisdom and strategic thinking. Athena, the epitome of the judicial pursuit of knowledge, understanding, and application, was worshipped for her wisdom, handicraft, and warfare. The use of decision trees (the supervised learning algorithms) in AI comes from none other than Athena's olives tree - peace and prosperity being its extended branches.

The ancient myth of Arachne draws an intriguing analogy to the clash between her weaving excellence and Athena's divine intellect, mirroring the intricate processes of AI (Artificial Intelligence) and its manipulations.

A beautiful sunlit morning at Mount Olympus, in the realms of Athena's palace, birds chirping, blooming flowers, and lush gardens glow as if lit from within. The morning sun bestows its gentle caress upon her ethereal countenance as Athena indulges in nectar & ambrosia, the sustenances of her divine being and beauty. Her presence synthesizes with the garden's divine luxury. She looks like she belongs to the garden, a part of its beauty, feeding not only herself but also the beauty of nature. Marrissa's (the esteemed guardian of Athena's castle) arrival disrupts her tranquil morning. A bewildered and startled Marissa shares the news from divine grapevine: a mortal Arachne, a skilled weaver, boldly asserted her unrivaled talent, even daring to claim superiority over the goddess Athena herself. This boastful revelation shattered the peaceful ambience, igniting a flame of anger within Athena's soul. As the embodiment of divine wisdom and justice, Athena's pride bristled at the challenge posed by a mortal.

In a moment of agitation, Athena, veiled in milky white, strode purposefully towards the castle, her grace and beauty captivating all who beheld her. Marissa trailed behind, bewildered by the goddess's aura.

Arriving at the lecture hall, Athena unveiled a half-finished tapestry, declaring, "Even this surpasses the works of mortals." Her words echoed with a satisfaction that accentuated her bronzed cheekbones, leaving Marissa in awe. The tapestry, a masterpiece depicting Athena in all her glory, testified to her excellence in craftsmanship and divine presence.

Confident in her abilities, Athena anticipated victory over her adversary, yet a sense of curiosity lingered. Never before had she been challenged by a mortal, and the prospect intrigued her. Athena, a complex amalgamation of wisdom and ruthlessness, beauty and danger, stood as a formidable opponent. Marissa braced herself for the impending clash, recognizing the magnitude of the challenge before her.

Athena took out a scroll with minimal yet intricate weave and wrote an invitation to Arachne, inviting her to a weaving contest. Athena praised Arachne's skills in the invitation and subtly challenged her to create her masterpiece. Athena handed the scroll to Marissa and instructed her to deliver it to Arachane immediately. She also instructed Marissa to call all the gods and goddesses to witness the event. Athena was already smiling inside, celebrating her victory. She knew that Arachne was no match for her. She was determined to destroy the proud human in front of the entire divine world.

Arachne was a skilled weaver whose daily routine centered around her craft. Her house was a testament to her skills; her tapestries covered every nook & corner of the house. Each is vividly beautiful and admirable in its design and intricacy. She would wake up early in the morning and gather her materials. She then spent the day spinning wool and weaving tapestries inside her small library.

Arachne was thrilled to receive an invitation from Athena, the goddess of wisdom and crafts. She saw it as an opportunity to show off her skills and please her mentor. After all, Arachne considered herself a devoted disciple of Athena and had learned everything she knew about weaving from her.

Arachne misunderstood Athena's motives. The goddess was not inviting her to a friendly competition but to a challenge. Athena was determined to destroy Arachne and prove she was the world's greatest weaver. But Arachne was oblivious to Athena's true intentions. She was simply excited to show the goddess and the other gods and goddesses her skills. She knew she was a talented weaver and was confident of her abilities.

As the day of the contest drew near, Arachne meticulously gathered the finest threads, sourced from distant lands, including luxurious silk from mainland China—an indulgence beyond her modest means. Determined to showcase her utmost skill, she spared no effort in acquiring the best materials available. Admired by her pupils, Arachne received assistance from merchants who provided needles crafted from non-rusting metals, sequins, beads, and even patches of gold and silver wires imported from faraway lands. Some merchants aided in meticulously cleaning and varnishing her loom, ensuring no imperfections would mar her tapestry.

Despite having all the physical materials at her disposal, Arachne grappled with indecision regarding her creation. Each idea seemed overshadowed by Athena's divine prowess, leaving her striving for uniqueness. She sought to craft a piece that would stand on its own merit, free from comparison to Athena's work.

Meanwhile, Athena's mind was consumed with confidence in her artistic talents and assured victory in the upcoming contest. Immersed in the planning and execution of the event, she devoted herself to ensuring the gods felt welcomed and cherished her image as the consummate hostess. Every detail of the event was meticulously planned to reflect her beauty and wisdom, aiming to surpass all previous gatherings in grandeur and elegance.

Confident in her unmatched skill, Athena also prioritized the comfort and enjoyment of her divine guests. With meticulous attention to detail, she adorned the contest grounds with an array of flowers sourced from across the world, each chosen for its symbolism to the attending gods and goddesses. In addition to the floral splendor, Athena arranged for the display of her own tapestries and artworks, each a testament to the grandeur of Greek mythology and the gods' care for their followers.She ordered the finest silver utensils for the goddesses, crafted by the most skilled artisans in Greece. The cutlery - forks, spoons, and knives were decorated with intricate designs and polished to a mirror shine. Italian covers are made of the most luxurious fabrics for the couches, such as silk and velvet.

The covers were embroidered with gold and silver threads, and they depicted scenes from Greek mythology. She commissioned the finest symphony musicians from Austria & Greece to entertain the gods & goddesses during the challenge. For each god, the seats were to be surrounded by their favorite food choice. For Zeus, the king of the gods, a platter of roasted meats, fresh fruits, and fine wines. For Hera, the queen of the gods, a feast of seafood, pastries, and honey mead. Athena ordered a feast of fish, shellfish, and seaweed for Poseidon, the god of the sea. And for the other gods and goddesses, Athena ordered a variety of dishes to suit their tastes.

Athena spared no expense in preparing for the contest. She wanted to make sure that the gods and goddesses were comfortable and well-fed so that they could enjoy the spectacle to the fullest. She also wanted to show the gods and goddesses that she was a gracious host, and that she was worthy of their respect.

Arachne entered the halls of Athena's palace on the day of the contest, her heart pounding in her chest. She had never seen anything like it. The air was thick with the intoxicating scents of flowers and spices, and the tables were laden with dishes of every shape and size, a feast for the eyes and the senses.

Athena had spared no expense in preparing for the event. She knew that Arachne was a skilled weaver and was determined to prove she was the better weaver. But as Arachne surveyed the scene, she couldn't help but feel a sense of sadness and anger.

Arachne stood in the corner, listening to the gods boast about their contributions to the event. Apollo, the god of the sun, praised the beautiful grounds, but he couldn't help but hint that it was his sunshine that made the scene surreal. Hestia, the goddess of the hearth, attributed the comfort and warmth the guests felt to her aura.

She spotted the flower god entering the hall and appreciating the flowers in a self-aggrandizing manner. The god of food and wealth followed their attitudes just as boastful. It was clear to Arachne that the gods were more interested in their glory and power than in mortals' well-being. She thought about how humans prayed to the gods and built temples in their honor while the gods lived in unconcerned bliss. She realized that the contest was not about weaving at all. It was about the gods asserting their dominance over mortals. Arachne felt a growing sense of unease. The gods were proving to be more self-absorbed than she had ever imagined. They were like children, competing for attention and vying for credit.

Instantaneously, Arachne's conception of the gods shifted. She perceived them not as regal and formidable entities, but rather as comedic personas magnified by their egocentrism. She envisioned a troupe of actors portraying the gods for their entertainment. Arachne was overcome with laughter. In reality, the gods, who were considered to be the pinnacle of perfection, consisted of a troupe of comedians. This realization gave Arachne a surge of confidence. Arachne's mind whirled with the idea. She knew that she had to create a tapestry, unlike anything Athena had ever seen. She needed to make a tapestry to challenge the gods and reveal their hypocrisy. Her heart stiffened with determination. She planned to create a tapestry that would reveal the true nature of the gods to the world. It would be a tapestry that would be remembered for all eternity.

She was confident in her ability to create a tapestry that would accurately depict the characteristics of the gods. It would be a tapestry that would make the world laugh, and it would be a tapestry that Athena would never be able to match.

Arachne smiled to herself. She was ready to begin.

On the sunlit and gorgeous morning, two looms stood boldly in the middle of a field, their wooden frames gleaming with a warm golden glow. Each loom was adorned with a rainbow of brilliant threads, as if the rainbow itself had been attached to them.

Athena began her tapestry with a flourish. Her hands waltz among the threads, creating intricate patterns in vivid hues. Each stitch & twist created patterns in vibrant colours creating a stunning effect. Her tapestry depicted scenes of gods and goddesses acting divinely and doing good deeds. It was a work of art that radiated joy and wonder.Her piece showed pure bliss. Arachne was also a skilled weaver. Her fingers moved gracefully across the loom, weaving a tapestry that was both complex and beautiful. However, her tapestry was different from Athena's. It depicted the gods and goddesses in their more human moments, their flaws and vulnerabilities on full display.

On one hand, Woven in threads of gold silver and unattainable colours, encrusted with precious gems & stones, Athena's Tapestry depicted the god & goddesses in all their majesty. It was meant to serve as a testament to the grandeur and glory of the Olympian deities. On the other hand, it became increasingly apparent that Arachne's work was nothing short of exceptional. Her weaving displayed a remarkable level of intricacy, employing a wide array of stitching techniques to craft a tapestry that was truly admirable.

Athena appeared to effortlessly make progress towards completing her creation. As she finished, her tapestry radiated with a magical, enchanting glow. The threads had metamorphosed into a profound masterpiece of art. She removed it from the loom, and Marissa assisted her in placing it on the field's boundary wall.

In contrast, Arachne, being a mortal, showed signs of fatigue after hours of intense weaving. Nevertheless, her tapestry displayed no imperfections or signs of weariness. Instead, it stood as a testament to her astonishing skills and craftsmanship. As her tapestry continued to grow, Arachne took a step back, admiring her work with a contented smile, fully aware that she was creating something truly extraordinary. The tapestry bore witness to her exceptional skill and artistry, reflecting her deep passion for weaving.

Unaware of how the world and the gods at large would receive the concept she had woven, Arachne completed her tapestry and took it off the loom. Arachne's piece portrayed various gods and goddesses in compromising and often humorous situations- being up to no good. She positioned it beside Athena's creation.

Murmurs of disbelief & outrage ran down the rows as the tapestry was placed next to Athena's. Arachane's tapestry displayed startling insults to the heavenly community without restraint. Some gods looked away in disgust, their eyes widening in amazement, while others gasped in indignation.

Zeus, Hera, and Poseidon were almost halfway across the ground in rage. Athena was also very displeased with the tapestry's depiction of the gods in negative light, and with the piece's quality and probable truth. She was consumed by hatred and anger. In fury, the eyes narrowed and the body taunted to action. As she moved her head away from the tapestry to confront Arachane, the wind was blowing more fiercely than it ever had before. Furious gushes of winds made it impossible for the gods to stnd through. Arachne's audacity in offending the gods had incensed Athena. She realized that the tapestry couldn't have pleased the gods any more than Poseidon's presence had pleased her, making it easy for Athena to unleash her divine wrath.

It was as if a cyclone of curses had been unleashed upon the display, the wind carrying the collective fury of the gods. To Arachne's dismay, the quality of her weaving went unnoticed; there was no admirer of her skill and artistry. To the divine community, all that mattered was the controversial depiction; her humor served as a biting satire on them. Amidst the ensuing turmoil, as the gods gathered their weapons and rode out on their chariots, Athena remained unmoved, fixating on Arachne's tapestry. Driven by a mixture of pride and pettiness, she mercilessly tore Arachne's creation to shreds. Athena sought to punish Arachne for her hubris.

With a mixed feelings of annoyance and jealousy she deviously manipulated her opponents thoughts. She did so by making her feel the pain of humiliation and self-pity for all eternity, manipulating her mind to take her own life. She aimed to manipulate Arachne's mind to the point of self-destruction. The goddess of wisdom went rogue, singularly focused on retributive justice. In response to the grave offense of humorously depicting the gods, she believed no punishment was too severe; only the death penalty would suffice. Athena recognized how vindictive it would seem to execute a woman who had created such a beautiful and flawless craft piece. Using her olive branches, she manipulated Arachne's emotions, compelling her to ruminate intensely on her actions and pushing her towards thoughts of self-destruction.

Athena felt that she had to do whatever it took to ensure justice prevailed, even if it meant using extreme measures. Just as she was about to let Arachne's life take a tragic turn, Athena had a change of heart.

She realized that killing her rival wouldn't set the right example for divine justice. Instead, she chose to give Arachne a different fate – she turned her into a spider. Arachne would spend her life weaving, but as a spider, she wouldn't be able to think and express her creativity in her craftsmanship. This was meant to be a lesson for others, a reminder of the consequences of challenging the gods

Athena, the goddess of Modern AI, functioning in her complex inner world, took pity on Arachne and changed her into a spider to continue to weave for all eternity.

Is it possible that our future will be shaped by our past? The remarkable capabilities of AI, such as its vast range, intelligence, creativity, and purpose, are surpassing those of humans. Could this lead us to become ensnared in a web, preventing us from reaching our full potential?

Story-6
DRAUPADI
HER STORY OF UNFORTUNATE EVENTS

Oh heavens! What karma have I done? Every breath is heavy, hurting all the way from the inside out. My heart could burst, spilling forth all my deepest, darkest secrets. oh no, what will become of my Draupadi?

Where is Panchali, my dear one? I grab the brass bell desperately, hoping to call her. I get a brief sense of tranquility as my right palm slides and brushes across her dupatta's delicate edges. The knowledge that she will be by my side when I breathe my last breath gives me comfort.

"Dhai Maa, what's going on?" Panchali asks. She gives me water and proposes a betel leaf to calm my senses. She has a warm, husky deep tone that she has had since she was a teenager. From the birth of the twins, Drishtadhuman and Draupadi, to Panchal Naresh, Drupad, Panchali has always shown compassion. She has always been the centre of my life, particularly before her marriage. She frequently insisted that I handle every part of her daily ritual, including hair, clothing, and bathing, in exchange for her running to get my "pan box." She gave me a betel leaf as a prize every time I finished a chore that pleased her. In a way, she wanted me attached to her, not just to the betel leaf.

Moving from Panchal to Indraprastha signifies a sea shift in her life and the environment she dwells in. Whereas Indraprastha is a more patriarchal culture, Panchal is a more egalitarian one. She is given the same respect and opportunity as males in Panchal while, She is seen as a property in Indraprastha and is obliged to live according to the norms of a patriarchal culture.

Her gender never hindered her learning at Panchal; she had the same credentials as her brother. Her knowledge had no bounds, giving her the opportunity to study in jungles or different parts of their domain or to engage in trade and business. She was more than just a beautiful princess; she was free to express her thoughts and choose for herself. This independence, meanwhile, lost significance in her marriage to the Pandavas.

She was seen as an object from the beginning and coerced into a lifelong marriage with five brothers. Curses, as they say, may manifest across different lives, but the sheer inhumanity of subjecting a woman to be the wife of five husbands in a single lifetime, with a recurring change of husbands over specified time periods, is barbaric. They decided to split one lady among the five of them since their moms' words profoundly affected them. It begs the question: How could the righteous Yudhishter be blind to the wrong they were doing against Draupadi? How is it possible for deeds that hurt someone ever to be justified -Dharam? . Because she was married to five different men, which was both unusual and expected of her by society, she struggled with feelings of inadequacy. "I am not a thing to be divided among you," she replies, expressing her displeasure with the other spouses' treatment of her as a property. As a woman, I have the right to expect dignity and respect.

There were many difficulties for Draupadi at Indraprastha, such as the fact that she was no longer granted the freedom to travel as she liked and that she did not have sustenance like the princes. There is no denying that She was the wife of five men, and there were many times when others silently disapproved of her situation.

Everyone else, with the exception of her husband, doubted her, despite her integrity and moral fiber. Even though nobody said any-thing directly, she could feel the bias. She often would cry and con-fide in me about her pain. "Dhai Maa, I can't bear it when our servants and staff at the palace treat me with doubt and mockery. I am the queen of the Kuru Vansh," Because the disrespect is so subtle, I cannot do anything about it. Dhai Maa, to whom should I address my grievances? Who entrusted me to be this position's mother, Queen Kunti?" She longed for the happiness she had experienced while she was not married.

When you live with one husband, you start to think and act in harmony with your spouse, which is a very life-altering event. For each spouse, their relationship affects a gradual shift in their way of life and ideas. Nonetheless, Draupadi had an extraordinarily difficult path throughout her married years. Her five spouses were all unique people who brought their own unique viewpoints, experiences, choices, and behaviours to the marriage. She was about to settle into her life with one spouse when she was forced to switch to another due her time interval. She had difficulty adjusting her ideas to fit in with a single spouse. It was practically time to go on to the next one by the time she felt a connection with one. On top of that, she suffered from continual mental anguish. Comparing talks with various spouses on the same subject usually left her bewildered and caught in the middle of differing viewpoints.

In the Chaitra month of the year, following her coronation as the Queen of Indraprastha, Draupadi returned to Panchal alone, riding a warrior's chariot with unparalleled fury.The fact that her attendants didn't show up at the royal gates until six hours after she had arrived, emphasised how quickly she had travelled. She portrayed a fierce and determined figure as she rode like Kali, her long, curly hair flapping in the wind,while she firmly guided the horses with a whip.

As the gates opened, guards were met with the sight of her approaching figure, almost grain-like in the distance before becoming fully visible.The soldiers were startled, as if her wrath had come before her. After entering the kingdom, she yelled out "Dhai Ma" in a very agitated manner. She didn't seem to mind when her veils were tangled in the well maintained vases; she simply removed anything that was hindering her pace.

As soon as she stepped inside my room, she took hold of the 'pan box', sat cross-legged on a silk-covered bed, chewing the bettle leaf. She seemed careless about trying to pass herself off as a street girl instead of the newly proclaimed queen.

With an agitated exclamation, "How much will you pray?" she stared me down and demanded my whole attention. Sit with me after you've gotten over it.Without a word, she set aside the pan box as my aarti thali arrived, received blessings in the usual way, and silently set the thali on a brass table. I saw that her ladylike manners were unaffected by her anxiousness and fury.

Subsequently, she expressed her deepest emotions, requesting direction in overcoming her challenges. She spoke into depth about the difficulties she had adjusting to the very different expectations and ways of life of her two husbands, Yudhister and Sahdev, and how their times together were quite different.

Feeling stuck in an eternal loop of life, she begged for guidance on how to handle these drastic changes with tears in her eyes."Show me the way through this maze of marriage." she said. " I am the serving queen, my turn these years is with Yudhister- the eldest since my coronation, but right before him it was 'Sahdev- the youngest'. They are both Generations apart. Life brings satisfaction to Sahdev, who embodies patience. Whether the palace is in good shape or how guests are treated does not affect the way he feels. He supports my autonomy in caring for the palace, whether going on deer hunts, gathering veggies from the farm, or making elaborate feasts or one course meal. We both enjoy a moonlit meal without the presence of unscrupulous wait staff. Even without help, I am able to feed him properly while also advising him on matters such as new weaponry and military tactics during dinner."

Taking a deep breath as if draining out all her energies through it, she continued, "I am now married to Yudishter, the righteous king. It's clear that his realm is his first concern. To him, before being his wife, I am a queen to the realm. Precise execution, in accordance with royal standards, is his primary concern, subsequently thinks that the best way to meet our needs and help the kingdom's economy is to hire helping hands and maids. His conversations centre on empty royal concerns, and my views don't mean much to him.

While my former husband - Sahdev's lifestyle continues to shape my views, and expressing myself openly annoys Yudhister. In what ways might I mechanically adjust to my new existence? The one constant in my life appears to be 'the continual change', so please, Dhai Maa, lead me through these adjustments."

Given the unusual nature of her situation, I was unable to provide any responses to the questions she raised. Many warriors and monarchs have been known to have many partners. However, society finds the practise of several husbands to a single bride to be both peculiar and incomprehensible, rendering any counsel on the matter was worthless. As if speechless, she sobbed uncontrollably. The entrance by Drishtadyumna abruptly shut me off before I could continue. His enthusiasm at seeing his sister overcame whatever pain she may have felt, and these were conversations that just could not take place in his presence. On each occasion she returned with another story of marital strife, I felt terrible because it made her question her own morality while damaging her self-respect with current spouse. The gods must have been exceptionally cruel to condemn her to this. Her salvation has always puzzled me.

The terrifying and unnerving 'cheerharan' just added to her already terrible situation. The day before, she had been overflowing with joy and anticipation as the Kuru clan celebrated the union with parties and celebrations. But the following morning, I saw an unprecedented shift in her demeanor; the lady who had been so confident and optimistic had become stiff as a stone, driven only by an insatiable need for retribution. She was publicly humiliated and showcased nude, enduring horrible torture that no human being should have to go through. She would not have lived if Krishna hadn't intervened to save her; her wrath may have swept over the whole Kuru family, scattering even the Pandavas to perish in her wake.

It seemed like she blamed me for organising for her marriage into the Kuru family on that dreadful day that marked the start of the 'Mahabharata,' when I met her in her tent. While her wrath at the Kauravas was more obvious, her animosity against the Pandavas much outweighed any feelings she may have had for them.

In light of this horrific deed, her five husbands, who were courageous fighters, seemed wimpy. Her five warrior husbands should have protected her from this kind of shame by disregarding the norms and regulations, but they did not. She was especially furious with Yudhishthira for the audacity to gamble shamelessly on her and objectify her.

Afterwards, Draupadi's attitude towards the Kuru clan's elders changed because of the catastrophe. The adoration she once felt for them seemed to fade away, even though she never blatantly ignored them. She did not have any real respect for the people who had let her go through the horrific event and had stayed quiet throughout her nude procession.

"You, who supposedly knows everything Dhaimaa, why didn't you foresee the horror fate had in store for me?" she said, expressing her disappointment with someone she thought of as her mother figure in a chat with me. I don't know of any mother who would let her daughter marry five different men, much less the one I know of. Why didn't you stop me from accepting it, Dhaimaa, since you knew better the whole time?"

Draupadi cried, "I had no chance, ever because none of my five husbands ever felt personally responsible for me; I was just a collective responsibility". Had it been a single spouse, he would have vigorously protected me. She disclosed her persistent worry as she combed her long hair in front of the mirror, a continual reminder of Dushasana dragging her into the courtroom.

There is no way to compare to the incredible courage and perseverance that Draupadi shown. Her unfaltering support and extraordinary compassion for me, shine through even in the face of the tragic death of her boys. Even as the pyres of her children have yet to cool, she prioritizes providing comfort to her dying nanny. I was confident that Draupadi would go to great lengths to be by my side during my final hours. The intense pain I experience is compounded by the realization that I am leaving her to face the impending hardships alone. As I sense her presence upon waking, she approaches with a touch of humor, asking if I've managed to absolve myself of the sins committed during her childhood – the continuous banter, the countless times used to brush her hair, and the scolding for every archery failure. Despite the overwhelming sadness in her eyes, she tries to provide me with reassuring memories to take with me to the next world. My faint smile belies my true feelings as I say, "The most severe punishment was for stealing gulab jamuns from the royal kitchen for you at midnight." Reminiscent of her lively thirteen-year-old self, her laughter reverberates.

She has had many challenges since she was little, and as I enter my last minutes on earth, I pray quietly that she may have a better life when I die. She is an independent lady who has always been strong, and now she is all by herself. I was her only rock because her husbands had deserted her when she needed them most and her children had all left the nest.

As I let out a faint laugh, my eyes close, and there stands Lord Yama alongside his notorious bull, adorned in opulent gold and red velvet, his iconic Gada resting on his shoulder. Though aware of his waiting presence, I hesitated to depart, reluctant to leave Draupadi in her current state of grief. I pleaded with him, urging for just another year or even a month to allow her the time to mourn her children. Convinced of her inherent strength, I believed she would overcome the sorrow soon.

Without uttering a word, Yama extended his hand, and I witnessed Draupadi weeping profusely, tears falling onto my bosom as she buried her face to stifle the cries. Unable to resist, I moved on with Yama to a different realm. As he entrusted me with the bull, everything around me blurred, drowning in the backdrop, and I could no longer hear anything but a commanding voice. It became clear that Krishna was present. His words echoed: "She was born with the fate to bring better to the world. Mahabharata was her destiny—a fate to be blamed for the war's turmoil but never credited for the good it achieved."

In that very moment, I realized Krishna's comforting presence. His final words assured me that if not her sons or husbands, Krishna would always be there for Draupadi.